Marissa V. 6th

The Epic of Gilgamesh

TRANSLATED BY N. K. SANDARS

PENGUIN EPICS

PENGUIN BOOKS

Published by the Penguin Group
Penguin Books Ltd, 80 Strand, London WC2R ORL, England
Penguin Group (USA) Inc., 375 Hudson Street, New York, New York 10014, USA
Penguin Group (Canada), 90 Eglinton Avenue East, Suite 700, Toronto, Ontario, Canada M4P 2Y3
(a division of Pearson Penguin Canada Inc.)
Penguin Ireland, 25 St Stephen's Green, Dublin 2, Ireland (a division of Penguin Books Ltd)
Penguin Group (Australia), 250 Camberwell Road, Camberwell, Victoria 3124, Australia
(a division of Pearson Australia Group Pty Ltd)
Penguin Books India Pvt Ltd, 11 Community Centre, Panchsheel Park, New Delhi – 110 017, India
Penguin Group (NZ), cnr Airborne and Rosedale Roads, Albany,
Auckland 1310, New Zealand (a division of Pearson New Zealand Ltd)
Penguin Books (South Africa) (Pty) Ltd, 24 Sturdee Avenue,
Rosebank, Johannesburg 2196, South Africa

Penguin Books Ltd, Registered Offices: 80 Strand, London WC2R ORL, England

www.penguin.com

This translation of *The Epic of Gilgamesh* first published 1960
Reprinted with revisions 1964
Reprinted with revisions 1972
This extract published in Penguin Books 2006

7

Translation copyright © N. K. Sandars, 1960, 1964, 1972
All rights reserved

Taken from the Penguin Classics edition of *The Epic of Gilgamesh*, translated by N. K. Sandars

Typeset by Rowland Phototypesetting Ltd, Bury St Edmunds, Suffolk
Printed in England by Clays Ltd, St Ives plc

ISBN–13: 978–0–141–02628–2

www.greenpenguin.co.uk

Mixed Sources
Product group from well-managed
forests and other controlled sources
www.fsc.org Cert no. SA COC-1592
© 1996 Forest Stewardship Council

Penguin Books is committed to a sustainable future
for our business, our readers and our planet.
The book in your hands is made from paper
certified by the Forest Stewardship Council.

Contents

Note

The Epic of Gilgamesh, which dates from the third millennium BC, is one of the finest, and oldest, surviving epic poems in world literature. It was miraculously preserved on clay tablets which were excavated in Mesopotamia in the nineteenth century. The poems centre round the character of the King Gilgamesh and his futile search for immortality. His arduous journey to the Spring of Youth, his friendship with Enkidu and his encounters with terrifying monsters and brutal gods create a mixture of pure adventure, tragedy and morality and make this ancient poem vividly alive to modern readers.

Gilgamesh King in Uruk

I will proclaim to the world the deeds of Gilgamesh. This was the man to whom all things were known; this was the king who knew the countries of the world. He was wise, he saw mysteries and knew secret things, he brought us a tale of the days before the flood. He went on a long journey, was weary, worn-out with labour, returning he rested, he engraved on a stone the whole story.

When the gods created Gilgamesh they gave him a perfect body. Shamash the glorious sun endowed him with beauty, Adad the god of the storm endowed him with courage, the great gods made his beauty perfect, surpassing all others, terrifying like a great wild bull. Two thirds they made him god and one third man.

In Uruk he built walls, a great rampart, and the temple of blessed Eanna for the god of the firmament Anu, and for Ishtar the goddess of love. Look at it still today: the outer wall where the cornice runs, it shines with the brilliance of copper; and the inner wall, it has no equal. Touch the threshold, it is ancient. Approach Eanna the dwelling of Ishtar, our lady of love and war, the like of which no latter-day king, no man alive can equal. Climb upon the wall of Uruk; walk along it, I say; regard the foundation terrace and examine the masonry: is it not burnt brick and good? The seven sages laid the foundations.

The Coming of Enkidu

Gilgamesh went abroad in the world, but he met with none who could withstand his arms till he came to Uruk. But the men of Uruk muttered in their houses, 'Gilgamesh sounds the tocsin for his amusement, his arrogance has no bounds by day or night. No son is left with his father, for Gilgamesh takes them all, even the children; yet the king should be a shepherd to his people. His lust leaves no virgin to her lover, neither the warrior's daughter nor the wife of the noble; yet this is the shepherd of the city, wise, comely, and resolute.'

The gods heard their lament, the gods of heaven cried to the Lord of Uruk, to Anu the god of Uruk: 'A goddess made him, strong as a savage bull, none can withstand his arms. No son is left with his father, for Gilgamesh takes them all; and is this the king, the shepherd of his people? His lust leaves no virgin to her lover, neither the warrior's daughter nor the wife of the noble.' When Anu had heard their lamentation the gods cried to Aruru, the goddess of creation, 'You made him, O Aruru, now create his equal; let it be as like him as his own reflection, his second self, stormy heart for stormy heart. Let them contend together and leave Uruk in quiet.'

So the goddess conceived an image in her mind, and it was of the stuff of Anu of the firmament. She dipped her hands in water and pinched off clay, she let it fall in the wilderness, and noble Enkidu was created. There was virtue in him of the god of war, of Ninurta himself. His body was rough, he had long hair like a woman's; it waved like the hair of Nisaba, the goddess of corn. His body was covered with matted hair like Samuqan's, the god of cattle. He was innocent of mankind; he knew nothing of the cultivated land.

Enkidu ate grass in the hills with the gazelle and lurked with wild beasts at the water-holes; he had joy of the water with the herds of wild game. But there was a trapper who met him one day face to face at the drinking-hole, for the wild game had entered his territory. On three days he met him face to face, and the trapper was frozen with fear. He went back to his house with the game that he had caught, and he was dumb, benumbed with terror. His face was altered like that of one who has made a long journey. With awe in his heart he spoke to his father: 'Father, there is a man, unlike any other, who comes down from the hills. He is the strongest in the world, he is like an immortal from heaven. He ranges over the hills with wild beasts and eats grass; he ranges through your land and comes down to the wells. I am afraid and dare not go near him. He fills in the pits which I dig and tears up my traps set for the game; he helps the beasts to escape and now they slip through my fingers.'

His father opened his mouth and said to the trapper, 'My son, in Uruk lives Gilgamesh; no one has ever prevailed against him, he is strong as a star from heaven. Go to Uruk, find Gilgamesh, extol the strength of this wild man. Ask him to give you a harlot, a wanton from the temple of love; return with her, and let her woman's power overpower this man. When next he comes down to drink at the wells she will be there, stripped naked; and when he sees her beckoning he will embrace her, and then the wild beasts will reject him.'

So the trapper set out on his journey to Uruk and addressed himself to Gilgamesh saying, 'A man unlike any other is roaming now in the pastures; he is as strong as a star from heaven and I am afraid to approach him. He helps the wild game to escape; he fills in my pits and pulls up my traps.' Gilgamesh said, 'Trapper, go back, take with you a harlot, a child of pleasure. At the drinking-hole she will strip, and when he sees her beckoning he will embrace her and the game of the wilderness will surely reject him.'

Now the trapper returned, taking the harlot with him. After a three days' journey they came to the drinking-hole, and there they sat down; the harlot and the trapper sat facing one another and waited for the game to come. For the first day and for the second day the two sat waiting, but on the third day the herds came; they came down to drink and Enkidu was with them. The small wild creatures of the plains were glad of the water, and Enkidu with them, who ate grass with the gazelle and was born in the hills; and she saw him, the savage man, come from far-off in the hills. The trapper spoke to her: 'There he is. Now, woman, make your breasts bare, have no shame, do not delay but welcome his love. Let him see you naked, let him possess your body. When he comes near uncover yourself and lie with him; teach him, the savage man, your woman's art, for when he murmurs love to you the wild beasts that shared his life in the hills will reject him.'

She was not ashamed to take him, she made herself naked and welcomed his eagerness; as he lay on her murmuring love she taught him the woman's art. For six days and seven nights they lay together, for Enkidu had forgotten his home in the hills; but when he was satisfied he went back to the wild beasts. Then, when the gazelle saw him, they bolted away; when the wild creatures saw him they fled. Enkidu would have followed, but his body was bound as though with a cord, his knees gave way when he started to run, his swiftness was gone. And now the wild creatures had all fled away; Enkidu was grown weak, for wisdom was in him, and the thoughts of a man were in his heart. So he returned and sat down at the woman's feet, and listened intently to what she said. 'You are wise, Enkidu, and now you have become like a god. Why do you want to run wild with the beasts in the hills? Come with me. I will take you to strong-walled Uruk, to the blessed temple of Ishtar and of Anu, of love and of heaven: there Gilgamesh lives, who is very strong, and like a wild bull he lords it over men.'

When she had spoken Enkidu was pleased; he longed for a comrade, for one who would understand his heart. 'Come, woman, and take me to that holy temple, to the house of Anu and of Ishtar, and to the place where Gilgamesh lords it over the people. I will challenge him boldly, I will cry out aloud in Uruk, "I am the strongest here, I have come to change the old order, I am he who was born in the hills, I am he who is strongest of all."'

She said, 'Let us go, and let him see your face. I know

very well where Gilgamesh is in great Uruk. O Enkidu, there all the people are dressed in their gorgeous robes, every day is holiday, the young men and the girls are wonderful to see. How sweet they smell! All the great ones are roused from their beds. O Enkidu, you who love life, I will show you Gilgamesh, a man of many moods; you shall look at him well in his radiant manhood. His body is perfect in strength and maturity; he never rests by night or day. He is stronger than you, so leave your boasting. Shamash the glorious sun has given favours to Gilgamesh, and Anu of the heavens, and Enlil, and Ea the wise has given him deep understanding. I tell you, even before you have left the wilderness, Gilgamesh will know in his dreams that you are coming.'

Now Gilgamesh got up to tell his dream to his mother, Ninsun, one of the wise gods. 'Mother, last night I had a dream. I was full of joy, the young heroes were round me and I walked through the night under the stars of the firmament, and one, a meteor of the stuff of Anu, fell down from heaven. I tried to lift it but it proved too heavy. All the people of Uruk came round to see it, the common people jostled and the nobles thronged to kiss its feet; and to me its attraction was like the love of woman. They helped me, I braced my forehead and I raised it with thongs and brought it to you, and you yourself pronounced it my brother.'

Then Ninsun, who is well-beloved and wise, said to Gilgamesh, 'This star of heaven which descended like a meteor from the sky; which you tried to lift, but found too heavy, when you tried to move it it would not budge, and so you brought it to my feet; I made it for you, a goad and spur, and you were drawn as though to a woman. This is the strong comrade, the one who brings help to his friend in his need. He is the strongest of wild creatures, the stuff of Anu; born in the grass-lands and the wild hills reared him; when you see him you will be glad; you will love him as a woman and he will never forsake you. This is the meaning of the dream.'

Gilgamesh said, 'Mother, I dreamed a second dream. In the streets of strong-walled Uruk there lay an axe; the shape of it was strange and the people thronged round. I saw it and was glad. I bent down, deeply drawn towards it; I loved it like a woman and wore it at my side.' Ninsun answered, 'That axe, which you saw, which drew you so powerfully like love of a woman, that is the comrade whom I give you, and he will come in his strength like one of the host of heaven. He is the brave companion who rescues his friend in necessity.' Gilgamesh said to his mother, 'A friend, a counsellor has come to me from Enlil, and now I shall befriend and counsel him.' So Gilgamesh told his dreams; and the harlot retold them to Enkidu.

And now she said to Enkidu, 'When I look at you you have become like a god. Why do you yearn to run wild again with the beasts in the hills? Get up from the ground, the bed of a shepherd.' He listened to her words with care. It was good advice that she gave. She divided her clothing in two and with the one half she clothed him and with the other herself; and holding his hand she led him like a child to the sheepfolds, into the shepherds' tents. There all the shepherds crowded round to see him, they put down bread in front of him, but Enkidu could only suck the milk of wild animals. He fumbled and

6

gaped, at a loss what to do or how he should eat the bread and drink the strong wine. Then the woman said, 'Enkidu, eat bread, it is the staff of life; drink the wine, it is the custom of the land.' So he ate till he was full and drank strong wine, seven goblets. He became merry, his heart exulted and his face shone. He rubbed down the matted hair of his body and anointed himself with oil. Enkidu had become a man; but when he had put on man's clothing he appeared like a bridegroom. He took arms to hunt the lion so that the shepherds could rest at night. He caught wolves and lions and the herdsmen lay down in peace; for Enkidu was their watchman, that strong man who had no rival.

He was merry living with the shepherds, till one day lifting his eyes he saw a man approaching. He said to the harlot, 'Woman, fetch that man here. Why has he come? I wish to know his name.' She went and called the man, saying, 'Sir, where are you going on this weary journey?' The man answered, saying to Enkidu, 'Gilgamesh has gone into the marriage-house and shut out the people. He does strange things in Uruk, the city of great streets. At the roll of the drum work begins for the men, and work for the women. Gilgamesh the king is about to celebrate marriage with the Queen of Love, and he still demands to be first with the bride, the king to be first and the husband to follow, for that was ordained by the gods from his birth, from the time the umbilical cord was cut. But now the drums roll for the choice of the bride and the city groans.' At these words Enkidu turned white in the face. 'I will go to the place where Gilgamesh lords it over the people, I will challenge him boldly, and

I will cry aloud in Uruk, "I have come to change the old order, for I am the strongest here." '

Now Enkidu strode in front and the woman followed behind. He entered Uruk, that great market, and all the folk thronged round him where he stood in the street in strong-walled Uruk. The people jostled; speaking of him they said, 'He is the spit of Gilgamesh.' 'He is shorter.' 'He is bigger of bone.' 'This is the one who was reared on the milk of wild beasts. His is the greatest strength.' The men rejoiced: 'Now Gilgamesh has met his match. This great one, this hero whose beauty is like a god, he is a match even for Gilgamesh.'

In Uruk the bridal bed was made, fit for the goddess of love. The bride waited for the bridegroom, but in the night Gilgamesh got up and came to the house. Then Enkidu stepped out, he stood in the street and blocked the way. Mighty Gilgamesh came on and Enkidu met him at the gate. He put out his foot and prevented Gilgamesh from entering the house, so they grappled, holding each other like bulls. They broke the doorposts and the walls shook, they snorted like bulls locked together. They shattered the doorposts and the walls shook. Gilgamesh bent his knee with his foot planted on the ground and with a turn Enkidu was thrown. Then immediately his fury died. When Enkidu was thrown he said to Gilgamesh, 'There is not another like you in the world. Ninsun, who is as strong as a wild ox in the byre, she was the mother who bore you, and now you are raised above all men, and Enlil has given you the kingship, for your strength surpasses the strength of men.' So Enkidu and Gilgamesh embraced and their friendship was sealed.

2

The Forest Journey

Enlil of the mountain, the father of the gods, had decreed the destiny of Gilgamesh. So Gilgamesh dreamed and Enkidu said, 'The meaning of the dream is this. The father of the gods has given you kingship, such is your destiny, everlasting life is not your destiny. Because of this do not be sad at heart, do not be grieved or oppressed. He has given you power to bind and to loose, to be the darkness and the light of mankind. He has given you unexampled supremacy over the people, victory in battle from which no fugitive returns, in forays and assaults from which there is no going back. But do not abuse this power, deal justly with your servants in the palace, deal justly before Shamash.'

The eyes of Enkidu were full of tears and his heart was sick. He sighed bitterly and Gilgamesh met his eye and said, 'My friend, why do you sigh so bitterly?' But Enkidu opened his mouth and said, 'I am weak, my arms have lost their strength, the cry of sorrow sticks in my throat, I am oppressed by idleness.' It was then that the lord Gilgamesh turned his thoughts to the Country of the Living; on the Land of Cedars the lord Gilgamesh reflected. He said to his servant Enkidu, 'I have not established my name stamped on bricks as my destiny decreed; therefore I will go to the country where the cedar is felled. I will set up my name in the place where the names of famous men are written, and where no man's name is written yet I will raise a monument to the gods. Because of the evil that is in the land, we will go to the forest and destroy the evil; for in the forest lives Humbaba whose name is "Hugeness", a ferocious giant.' But Enkidu sighed bitterly and said, 'When I went with the wild beasts ranging through the wilderness I discovered the forest; its length is ten thousand leagues in every direction. Enlil has appointed Humbaba to guard it and armed him in sevenfold terrors, terrible to all flesh is Humbaba. When he roars it is like the torrent of the storm, his breath is like fire, and his jaws are death itself. He guards the cedars so well that when the wild heifer stirs in the forest, though she is sixty leagues distant, he hears her. What man would willingly walk into that country and explore its depths? I tell you, weakness overpowers whoever goes near it: it is not an equal struggle when one fights with Humbaba; he is a great warrior, a battering-ram. Gilgamesh, the watchman of the forest never sleeps.'

Gilgamesh replied: 'Where is the man who can clamber to heaven? Only the gods live for ever with glorious Shamash, but as for us men, our days are numbered, our occupations are a breath of wind. How is this, already you are afraid! I will go first although I am your lord, and you may safely call out, "Forward, there is nothing to fear!" Then if I fall I leave behind me a name that endures; men will say of me, "Gilgamesh has fallen in fight with ferocious Humbaba." Long after the child has been born in my house, they will say it, and remember.' Enkidu spoke again to Gilgamesh, 'O my lord, if you will enter that country, go first to the hero Shamash, tell the Sun God, for the land is his. The country where the cedar is cut belongs to Shamash.'

Gilgamesh took up a kid, white without spot, and a brown one with it; he held them against his breast, and he carried them into the presence of the sun. He took in his hand his silver sceptre and he said to glorious Shamash, 'I am going to that country, O Shamash, I am going; my hands supplicate, so let it be well with my soul and bring me back to the quay of Uruk. Grant, I beseech, your protection, and let the omen be good.' Glorious Shamash answered, 'Gilgamesh, you are strong, but what is the Country of the Living to you?'

'O Shamash, hear me, hear me, Shamash, let my voice be heard. Here in the city man dies oppressed at heart, man perishes with despair in his heart. I have looked over the wall and I see the bodies floating on the river, and that will be my lot also. Indeed I know it is so, for whoever is tallest among men cannot reach the heavens, and the greatest cannot encompass the earth. Therefore I would enter that country: because I have not established my name stamped on brick as my destiny decreed, I will go to the country where the cedar is cut. I will set up my name where the names of famous men are written; and where no man's name is written I will raise a monument to the gods.' The tears ran down his face and he said, 'Alas, it is a long journey that I must take to the Land of Humbaba. If this enterprise is not to be accomplished, why did you move me, Shamash, with the restless desire to perform it? How can I succeed if you will not succour me? If I die in that country I will die without rancour, but if I return I will make a glorious offering of gifts and of praise to Shamash.'

So Shamash accepted the sacrifice of his tears; like the compassionate man he showed him mercy. He appointed strong allies for Gilgamesh, sons of one mother, and stationed them in the mountain caves. The great winds he appointed: the north wind, the whirlwind, the storm and the icy wind, the tempest and the scorching wind. Like vipers, like dragons, like a scorching fire, like a serpent that freezes the heart, a destroying flood and the lightning's fork, such were they and Gilgamesh rejoiced.

He went to the forge and said, 'I will give orders to the armourers; they shall cast us our weapons while we watch them.' So they gave orders to the armourers and the craftsmen sat down in conference. They went into the groves of the plain and cut willow and box-wood; they cast for them axes of nine score pounds, and great swords they cast with blades of six score pounds each one, with pommels and hilts of thirty pounds. They cast for Gilgamesh the axe 'Might of Heroes' and the bow of Anshan; and Gilgamesh was armed and Enkidu; and the weight of the arms they carried was thirty score pounds.

The people collected and the counsellors in the streets and in the market-place of Uruk; they came through the gate of seven bolts and Gilgamesh spoke to them in the market-place: 'I, Gilgamesh, go to see that creature of whom such things are spoken, the rumour of whose name fills the world. I will conquer him in his cedar wood and show the strength of the sons of Uruk, all the world shall know of it. I am committed to this enterprise: to climb the mountain, to cut down the cedar, and leave behind me an enduring name.' The counsellors of Uruk, the great market, answered him, 'Gilgamesh, you are young, your courage carries you too far, you cannot know what this enterprise means which you plan. We have heard that Humbaba is not like men who die, his weapons are such that none can stand against them; the forest stretches for ten thousand leagues in every direction; who would willingly go down to explore its depths? As for Humbaba, when he roars it is like the torrent of the storm, his breath is like fire and his jaws are death itself. Why do you crave to do this thing, Gilgamesh? It is no equal struggle when one fights with Humbaba, that battering-ram.'

When he heard these words of the counsellors Gilgamesh looked at his friend and laughed, 'How shall I answer them; shall I say I am afraid of Humbaba, I will sit at home all the rest of my days?' Then Gilgamesh opened his mouth again and said to Enkidu, 'My friend, let us go to the Great Palace, to Egalmah, and stand before Ninsun the queen. Ninsun is wise with deep knowledge, she will give us counsel for the road we must go.' They took each other by the hand as they went to Egalmah, and they went to Ninsun the great queen. Gilgamesh approached, he entered the palace and spoke to Ninsun. 'Ninsun, will you listen to me; I have a long journey to go, to the Land of Humbaba, I must travel an unknown road and fight a strange battle. From the day I go until I return, till I reach the cedar forest and destroy the evil which Shamash abhors, pray for me to Shamash.'

Ninsun went into her room, she put on a dress becoming to her body, she put on jewels to make her breast beautiful, she placed a tiara on her head and her skirts swept the ground. Then she went up to the altar of the Sun, standing upon the roof of the palace; she burnt incense and lifted her arms to Shamash as the smoke ascended: 'O Shamash, why did you give this restless heart to Gilgamesh, my son; why did you give it? You have moved him and now he sets out on a long journey to the Land of Humbaba, to travel an unknown road and fight a strange battle. Therefore from the day that he goes till the day he returns, until he reaches the cedar forest, until he kills Humbaba and destroys the evil thing which you, Shamash, abhor, do not forget him; but let the dawn, Aya, your dear bride, remind you always, and when day is done give him to the watchman of the night to keep him from harm.' Then Ninsun the mother of Gilgamesh extinguished the incense, and she called to Enkidu with this exhortation: 'Strong Enkidu, you are not the child of my body, but I will receive you as my adopted son; you are my other child like the foundlings they bring to the temple. Serve Gilgamesh as a foundling serves the temple and the priestess who reared him. In the presence of my women, my votaries and hierophants, I declare it.' Then she placed the amulet for a pledge round his neck, and she said to him, 'I entrust my son to you; bring him back to me safely.'

And now they brought to them the weapons, they put in their hands the great swords in their golden scabbards, and the bow and the quiver. Gilgamesh took the axe, he slung the quiver from his shoulder, and the bow of Anshan, and buckled the sword to his belt; and so they were armed and ready for the journey. Now all the people came and pressed on them and said, 'When will you return to the city?' The counsellors blessed Gilgamesh and warned him, 'Do not trust too much in your own strength, be watchful, restrain your blows at first. The one who goes in front protects his companion; the good guide who knows the way guards his friend. Let Enkidu lead the way, he knows the road to the forest, he has seen Humbaba and is experienced in battles; let him press first into the passes, let him be watchful and look to himself. Let Enkidu protect his friend, and guard his companion, and bring him safe through the pitfalls of the road. We, the counsellors of Uruk entrust our king to you, O Enkidu; bring him back safely to us.' Again to Gilgamesh they said, 'May Shamash give you your heart's desire, may he let you see with your eyes the thing accomplished which your lips have spoken; may he open a path for you where it is blocked, and a road for your feet to tread. May he open the mountains for your crossing, and may the night-time bring you the blessings of night, and Lugulbanda, your guardian god, stand beside you for victory. May you have victory in the battle as though you fought with a child. Wash your feet in the river of Humbaba to which you are journeying; in the evening dig a well, and let there always be pure water in your water-skin. Offer cold water to Shamash and do not forget Lugulbanda.'

Then Enkidu opened his mouth and said, 'Forward, there is nothing to fear. Follow me, for I know the place where Humbaba lives and the paths where he walks. Let the counsellors go back. Here is no cause for fear.' When the counsellors heard this they sped the hero on his way.

'Go, Gilgamesh, may your guardian god protect you on the road and bring you safely back to the quay of Uruk.'

After twenty leagues they broke their fast; after another thirty leagues they stopped for the night. Fifty leagues they walked in one day; in three days they had walked as much as a journey of a month and two weeks. They crossed seven mountains before they came to the gate of the forest. Then Enkidu called out to Gilgamesh, 'Do not go down into the forest; when I opened the gate my hand lost its strength.' Gilgamesh answered him, 'Dear friend, do not speak like a coward. Have we got the better of so many dangers and travelled so far, to turn back at last? You, who are tried in wars and battles, hold close to me now and you will feel no fear of death; keep beside me and your weakness will pass, the trembling will leave your hand. Would my friend rather stay behind? No, we will go down together into the heart of the forest. Let your courage be roused by the battle to come; forget death and follow me, a man resolute in action, but one who is not foolhardy. When two go together each will protect himself and shield his companion, and if they fall they leave an enduring name.'

Together they went down into the forest and they came to the green mountain. There they stood still, they were struck dumb; they stood still and gazed at the forest. They saw the height of the cedar, they saw the way into the forest and the track where Humbaba was used to walk. The way was broad and the going was good. They gazed at the mountain of cedars, the dwelling-place of the gods and the throne of Ishtar. The hugeness of the cedar rose in front of the mountain, its shade was beautiful, full of comfort; mountain and glade were green with brushwood.

There Gilgamesh dug a well before the setting sun. He went up the mountain and poured out fine meal on the ground and said, 'O mountain, dwelling of the gods, bring me a favourable dream.' Then they took each other by the hand and lay down to sleep; and sleep that flows from the night lapped over them. Gilgamesh dreamed, and at midnight sleep left him, and he told his dream to his friend. 'Enkidu, what was it that woke me if you did not? My friend, I have dreamed a dream. Get up, look at the mountain precipice. The sleep that the gods sent me is broken. Ah, my friend, what a dream I have had! Terror and confusion; I seized hold of a wild bull in the wilderness. It bellowed and beat up the dust till the whole sky was dark, my arm was seized and my tongue bitten. I fell back on my knee; then someone refreshed me with water from his water-skin.'

Enkidu said, 'Dear friend, the god to whom we are travelling is no wild bull, though his form is mysterious. That wild bull which you saw is Shamash the Protector; in our moment of peril he will take our hands. The one who gave water from his water-skin, that is your own god who cares for your good name, your Lugulbanda. United with him, together we will accomplish a work the fame of which will never die.'

Gilgamesh said, 'I dreamed again. We stood in a deep gorge of the mountain, and beside it we two were like the smallest of swamp flies; and suddenly the mountain fell, it struck me and caught my feet from under me. Then came an intolerable light blazing out, and in it was one whose grace and whose beauty were greater than the beauty of this world. He pulled me out from under the mountain, he gave me water to drink and my heart was comforted, and he set my feet on the ground.'

Then Enkidu the child of the plains said, 'Let us go down from the mountain and talk this thing over together.' He said to Gilgamesh the young god, 'Your dream is good, your dream is excellent, the mountain which you saw is Humbaba. Now, surely, we will seize and kill him, and throw his body down as the mountain fell on the plain.'

The next day after twenty leagues they broke their fast, and after another thirty they stopped for the night. They dug a well before the sun had set and Gilgamesh ascended the mountain. He poured out fine meal on the ground and said, 'O mountain, dwelling of the gods, send a dream for Enkidu, make him a favourable dream.' The mountain fashioned a dream for Enkidu; it came, an ominous dream; a cold shower passed over him, it caused him to cower like the mountain barley under a storm of rain. But Gilgamesh sat with his chin on his knees till the sleep which flows over all mankind lapped over him. Then, at midnight, sleep left him; he got up and said to his friend, 'Did you call me, or why did I wake? Did you touch me, or why am I terrified? Did not some god pass by, for my limbs are numb with fear? My friend, I saw a third dream and this dream was altogether frightful. The heavens roared and the earth roared again, daylight failed and darkness fell, lightnings flashed, fire blazed out, the clouds lowered, they rained down death. Then the brightness departed, the fire went out, and all was turned to ashes fallen about us. Let us go down from the mountain and talk this over, and consider what we should do.'

When they had come down from the mountain Gilgamesh seized the axe in his hand: he felled the cedar. When Humbaba heard the noise far off he was enraged; he cried out, 'Who is this that has violated my woods and cut down my cedar?' But glorious Shamash called to them out of heaven, 'Go forward, do not be afraid.' But now Gilgamesh was overcome by weakness, for sleep had seized him suddenly, a profound sleep held him; he lay on the ground, stretched out speechless, as though in a dream. When Enkidu touched him he did not rise, when he spoke to him he did not reply. 'O Gilgamesh, Lord of the plain of Kullab, the world grows dark, the shadows have spread over it, now is the glimmer of dusk. Shamash has departed, his bright head is quenched in the bosom of his mother Ningal. O Gilgamesh, how long will you lie like this, asleep? Never let the mother who gave you birth be forced in mourning into the city square.'

At length Gilgamesh heard him; he put on his breast-plate, 'The Voice of Heroes', of thirty shekels' weight; he put it on as though it had been a light garment that he carried, and it covered him altogether. He straddled the earth like a bull that snuffs the ground and his teeth were clenched. 'By the life of my mother Ninsun who gave me birth, and by the life of my father, divine Lugulbanda, let me live to be the wonder of my mother, as when she nursed me on her lap.' A second time he said to him, 'By the life of Ninsun my mother who gave me birth, and by the life of my father, divine Lugulbanda, until we have fought this man, if man he is, this god, if god he is, the way that I took to the Country of the Living will not turn back to the city.'

Then Enkidu, the faithful companion, pleaded, answering him, 'O my lord, you do not know this monster and that is the reason you are not afraid. I who know him, I am terrified. His teeth are dragon's fangs, his countenance is like a lion, his charge is the rushing of the flood, with his look he crushes alike the trees of the forest and reeds in the swamp. O my Lord, you may go on if you choose into this land, but I will go back to the city. I will tell the lady your mother all your glorious deeds till she shouts for joy: and then I will tell the death that followed till she weeps for bitterness.' But Gilgamesh said, 'Immolation and sacrifice are not yet for me, the boat of the dead shall not go down, nor the three-ply cloth be cut for my shrouding. Not yet will my people be desolate, nor the pyre be lit in my house and my dwelling burnt on the fire. Today, give me your aid and you shall have mine: what then can go amiss with us two? All living creatures born of the flesh shall sit at last in the boat of the West, and when it sinks, when the boat of Magilum sinks, they are gone; but we shall go forward and fix our eyes on this monster. If your heart is fearful throw away fear; if there is terror in it throw away terror. Take your axe in your hand and attack. He who leaves the fight unfinished is not at peace.'

Humbaba came out from his strong house of cedar. Then Enkidu called out, 'O Gilgamesh, remember now your boasts in Uruk. Forward, attack, son of Uruk, there is nothing to fear.' When he heard these words his courage rallied; he answered, 'Make haste, close in, if the watchman is there do not let him escape to the woods where he will vanish. He has put on the first of his seven splendours but not yet the other six, let us trap him before he is armed.' Like a raging wild bull he snuffed the ground; the watchman of the woods turned full of threatenings, he cried out. Humbaba came from his strong house of cedar. He nodded his head and shook it, menacing Gilgamesh; and on him he fastened his eye, the eye of death. Then Gilgamesh called to Shamash and his tears were flowing, 'O glorious Shamash, I have followed the road you commanded but now if you send no succour how shall I escape?' Glorious Shamash heard his prayer and he summoned the great wind, the north wind, the whirlwind, the storm and the icy wind, the tempest and the scorching wind; they came like dragons, like a scorching fire, like a serpent that freezes the heart, a destroying flood and the lightning's fork. The eight winds rose up against Humbaba, they beat against his eyes; he was gripped, unable to go forward or back. Gilgamesh shouted, 'By the life of Ninsun my mother and divine Lugulbanda my father, in the Country of the Living, in this Land I have discovered your dwelling; my weak arms and my small weapons I have brought to this Land against you, and now I will enter your house.'

So he felled the first cedar and they cut the branches and laid them at the foot of the mountain. At the first stroke Humbaba blazed out, but still they advanced. They felled seven cedars and cut and bound the branches and laid them at the foot of the mountain, and seven times Humbaba loosed his glory on them. As the seventh blaze died out they reached his lair. He slapped his thigh in scorn. He approached like a noble wild bull roped on the mountain, a warrior whose elbows are bound together. The tears started to his eyes and he was pale, 'Gilgamesh, let me speak. I have never known a mother, no, nor a father who reared me. I was born of the mountain, he reared me, and Enlil made me the keeper of this forest. Let me go free, Gilgamesh, and I will be your servant, you shall be my lord; all the trees of the forest that I tended on the mountain shall be yours. I will cut them down and build you a palace.' He took him by the hand and led him to his house, so that the heart of Gilgamesh was moved with compassion. He swore by the heavenly life, by the earthly life, by the underworld itself: 'O Enkidu, should not the snared bird return to its nest and the captive man return to his mother's arms?' Enkidu answered, 'The strongest of men will fall to fate if he has no judgement. Namtar, the evil fate that knows no distinction between men, will devour him. If the snared bird returns to its nest, if the captive man returns to his mother's arms, then you my friend will never return to the city where the mother is waiting who gave you birth. He will bar the mountain road against you, and make the pathways impassable.'

Humbaba said, 'Enkidu, what you have spoken is evil: you, a hireling, dependent for your bread! In envy and for fear of a rival you have spoken evil words.' Enkidu said, 'Do not listen, Gilgamesh: this Humbaba must die. Kill Humbaba first and his servants after.' But Gilgamesh said, 'If we touch him the blaze and the glory of light will be put out in confusion, the glory and glamour will vanish, its rays will be quenched.' Enkidu said to Gilgamesh, 'Not so, my friend. First entrap the bird, and where shall the chicks run then? Afterwards we can search out the glory and the glamour, when the chicks run distracted through the grass.'

Gilgamesh listened to the word of his companion, he took the axe in his hand, he drew the sword from his belt, and he struck Humbaba with a thrust of the sword to the neck, and Enkidu his comrade struck the second blow. At the third blow Humbaba fell. Then there followed confusion, for this was the guardian of the forest whom they had felled to the ground. For as far as two leagues the cedars shivered when Enkidu felled the watcher of the forest, he at whose voice Hermon and Lebanon used to tremble. Now the mountains were moved and all the hills, for the guardian of the forest was killed. They attacked the cedars, the seven splendours of Humbaba were extinguished. So they pressed on into the forest bearing the sword of eight talents. They uncovered the sacred dwellings of the Anunnaki and while Gilgamesh felled the first of the trees of the forest Enkidu cleared their roots as far as the banks of Euphrates. They set Humbaba before the gods, before Enlil; they kissed the ground and dropped the shroud and set the head before him. When he saw the head of Humbaba, Enlil raged at them, 'Why did you do this thing? From henceforth may the fire be on your faces, may it eat the bread that you eat, may it drink where you drink.' Then Enlil took again the blaze and the seven splendours that had been Humbaba's: he gave the first to the river, and he gave to the lion, to the stone of execration, to the mountain and to the dreaded daughter of the Queen of Hell.

O Gilgamesh, king and conqueror of the dreadful blaze; wild bull who plunders the mountain, who crosses the sea, glory to him, and from the brave the greater glory is Enki's!

3

Ishtar and Gilgamesh, and the Death of Enkidu

Gilgamesh washed out his long locks and cleaned his weapons; he flung back his hair from his shoulders; he threw off his stained clothes and changed them for new. He put on his royal robes and made them fast. When Gilgamesh had put on the crown, glorious Ishtar lifted her eyes, seeing the beauty of Gilgamesh. She said, 'Come to me Gilgamesh, and be my bridegroom; grant me seed of your body, let me be your bride and you shall be my husband. I will harness for you a chariot of lapis lazuli and of gold, with wheels of gold and horns of copper; and you shall have mighty demons of the storm for draft-mules. When you enter our house in the fragrance of cedar-wood, threshold and throne will kiss your feet. Kings, rulers, and princes will bow down before you; they shall bring you tribute from the mountains and the plain. Your ewes shall drop twins and your goats triplets; your pack-ass shall outrun mules; your oxen shall have no rivals, and your chariot horses shall be famous far-off for their swiftness.'

Gilgamesh opened his mouth and answered glorious Ishtar, 'If I take you in marriage, what gifts can I give in return? What ointments and clothing for your body? I would gladly give you bread and all sorts of food fit for a god. I would give you wine to drink fit for a queen. I would pour out barley to stuff your granary; but as for making you my wife – that I will not. How would it go with me? Your lovers have found you like a brazier which smoulders in the cold, a backdoor which keeps out neither squall of wind nor storm, a castle which crushes the garrison, pitch that blackens the bearer, a water-skin that chafes the carrier, a stone which falls from the parapet, a battering-ram turned back from the enemy, a sandal that trips the wearer. Which of your lovers did you ever love for ever? What shepherd of yours has pleased you for all time? Listen to me while I tell the tale of your lovers. There was Tammuz, the lover of your youth, for him you decreed wailing, year after year. You loved the many-coloured roller, but still you struck and broke his wing; now in the grove he sits and cries, "kappi, kappi, my wing, my wing." You have loved the lion tremendous in strength: seven pits you dug for him, and seven. You have loved the stallion magnificent in battle, and for him you decreed whip and spur and a thong, to gallop seven leagues by force and to muddy the water before he drinks; and for his mother Silili lamentations. You have loved the shepherd of the flock; he made meal-cake for you day after day, he killed kids for your sake. You struck and turned him into a wolf; now his own herd-boys chase him away, his own hounds worry his flanks. And did you not love Ishullanu, the gardener of your father's palm-grove? He brought you baskets filled with dates without end; every day he loaded your table. Then you turned your eyes on him and said, "Dearest Ishullanu, come here to me, let us enjoy

your manhood, come forward and take me, I am yours."
Ishullanu answered, "What are you asking from me? My
mother has baked and I have eaten; why should I come
to such as you for food that is tainted and rotten? For
when was a screen of rushes sufficient protection from
frosts?" But when you had heard his answer you struck
him. He was changed to a blind mole deep in the earth,
one whose desire is always beyond his reach. And if you
and I should be lovers, should not I be served in the
same fashion as all these others whom you loved once?'

When Ishtar heard this she fell into a bitter rage, she
went up to high heaven. Her tears poured down in front
of her father Anu, and Antum her mother. She said, 'My
father, Gilgamesh has heaped insults on me, he has told
over all my abominable behaviour, my foul and hideous
acts.' Anu opened his mouth and said, 'Are you a father
of gods? Did not you quarrel with Gilgamesh the king,
so now he has related your abominable behaviour, your
foul and hideous acts.'

Ishtar opened her mouth and said again, 'My father,
give me the Bull of Heaven to destroy Gilgamesh. Fill
Gilgamesh, I say, with arrogance to his destruction; but
if you refuse to give me the Bull of Heaven I will break
in the doors of hell and smash the bolts; there will be
confusion of people, those above with those from the
lower depths. I shall bring up the dead to eat food like
the living; and the hosts of dead will outnumber the
living.' Anu said to great Ishtar, 'If I do what you desire
there will be seven years of drought throughout Uruk
when corn will be seedless husks. Have you saved grain
enough for the people and grass for the cattle?' Ishtar

replied, 'I have saved grain for the people, grass for the cattle; for seven years of seedless husks there is grain and there is grass enough.'

When Anu heard what Ishtar had said he gave her the Bull of Heaven to lead by the halter down to Uruk. When they reached the gates of Uruk the Bull went to the river; with his first snort cracks opened in the earth and a hundred young men fell down to death. With his second snort cracks opened and two hundred fell down to death. With his third snort cracks opened, Enkidu doubled over but instantly recovered, he dodged aside and leapt on the Bull and seized it by the horns. The Bull of Heaven foamed in his face, it brushed him with the thick of its tail. Enkidu cried to Gilgamesh, 'My friend, we boasted that we would leave enduring names behind us. Now thrust in your sword between the nape and the horns.' So Gilgamesh followed the Bull, he seized the thick of its tail, he thrust the sword between the nape and the horns and slew the Bull. When they had killed the Bull of Heaven they cut out its heart and gave it to Shamash, and the brothers rested.

But Ishtar rose up and mounted the great wall of Uruk; she sprang on to the tower and uttered a curse: 'Woe to Gilgamesh, for he has scorned me in killing the Bull of Heaven.' When Enkidu heard these words he tore out the Bull's right thigh and tossed it in her face, saying, 'If I could lay my hands on you, it is this I should do to you, and lash the entrails to your side.' Then Ishtar called together her people, the dancing and singing girls, the prostitutes of the temple, the courtesans. Over the thigh of the Bull of Heaven she set up lamentation.

But Gilgamesh called the smiths and the armourers, all of them together. They admired the immensity of the horns. They were plated with lapis lazuli two fingers thick. They were thirty pounds each in weight, and their capacity in oil was six measures, which he gave to his guardian god, Lugulbanda. But he carried the horns into the palace and hung them on the wall. Then they washed their hands in Euphrates, they embraced each other and went away. They drove through the streets of Uruk where the heroes were gathered to see them, and Gilgamesh called to the singing girls, 'Who is most glorious of the heroes, who is most eminent among men?' 'Gilgamesh is the most glorious of heroes, Gilgamesh is most eminent among men.' And now there was feasting, and celebrations and joy in the palace, till the heroes lay down, saying, 'Now we will rest for the night.'

When the daylight came Enkidu got up and cried to Gilgamesh, 'O my brother, such a dream I had last night. Anu, Enlil, Ea and heavenly Shamash took counsel together, and Anu said to Enlil, "Because they have killed the Bull of Heaven, and because they have killed Humbaba who guarded the Cedar Mountain one of the two must die." Then glorious Shamash answered the hero Enlil, "It was by your command they killed the Bull of Heaven, and killed Humbaba, and must Enkidu die although innocent?" Enlil flung round in rage at glorious Shamash, "You dare to say this, you who went about with them every day like one of themselves!"'

So Enkidu lay stretched out before Gilgamesh; his tears ran down in streams and he said to Gilgamesh, 'O my brother, so dear as you are to me, brother, yet they will take me from you.' Again he said, 'I must sit down on the threshold of the dead and never again will I see my dear brother with my eyes.'

While Enkidu lay alone in his sickness he cursed the gate as though it was living flesh, 'You there, wood of the gate, dull and insensible, witless, I searched for you over twenty leagues until I saw the towering cedar. There is no wood like you in our land. Seventy-two cubits high and twenty-four wide, the pivot and the ferrule and the jambs are perfect. A master craftsman from Nippur has made you; but O, if I had known the conclusion! If I had known that this was all the good that would come of it, I would have raised the axe and split you into little pieces and set up here a gate of wattle instead. Ah, if only some future king had brought you here, or some god had fashioned you. Let him obliterate my name and write his own, and the curse fall on him instead of on Enkidu.'

With the first brightening of dawn Enkidu raised his head and wept before the Sun God, in the brilliance of the sunlight his tears streamed down. 'Sun God, I beseech you, about that vile Trapper, that Trapper of nothing because of whom I was to catch less than my comrade; let him catch least, make his game scarce, make him feeble, taking the smaller of every share, let his quarry escape from his nets.'

When he had cursed the Trapper to his heart's content he turned on the harlot. He was roused to curse her also. 'As for you, woman, with a great curse I curse you! I will promise you a destiny to all eternity. My curse shall come on you soon and sudden. You shall be without a roof for your commerce, for you shall not keep house with other girls in the tavern, but do your business in places fouled by the vomit of the drunkard. Your hire will be potter's earth, your thievings will be flung into the hovel, you will sit at the cross-roads in the dust of the potter's quarter, you will make your bed on the dunghill at night, and by day take your stand in the wall's shadow. Brambles and thorns will tear your feet, the drunk and the dry will strike your cheek and your mouth will ache. Let you be stripped of your purple dyes, for I too once in the wilderness with my wife had all the treasure I wished.'

When Shamash heard the words of Enkidu he called to him from heaven: 'Enkidu, why are you cursing the woman, the mistress who taught you to eat bread fit for gods and drink wine of kings? She who put upon you a magnificent garment, did she not give you glorious Gilgamesh for your companion, and has not Gilgamesh, your own brother, made you rest on a royal bed and recline on a couch at his left hand? He has made the princes of the earth kiss your feet, and now all the people of Uruk lament and wail over you. When you are dead he will let his hair grow long for your sake, he will wear a lion's pelt and wander through the desert.'

When Enkidu heard glorious Shamash his angry heart grew quiet, he called back the curse and said, 'Woman, I promise you another destiny. The mouth which cursed you shall bless you! Kings, princes and nobles shall adore you. On your account a man though twelve miles off will clap his hand to his thigh and his hair will twitch. For you he will undo his belt and open his treasure and you shall have your desire; lapis lazuli, gold and carnelian from the heap in the treasury. A ring for your hand and a robe shall be yours. The priest will lead you into the presence of the gods. On your account a wife, a mother of seven, was forsaken.'

As Enkidu slept alone in his sickness, in bitterness of spirit he poured out his heart to his friend. 'It was I who cut down the cedar, I who levelled the forest, I who slew Humbaba and now see what has become of me. Listen, my friend, this is the dream I dreamed last night. The heavens roared, and earth rumbled back an answer; between them stood I before an awful being, the sombre-faced man-bird; he had directed on me his purpose. His was a vampire face, his foot was a lion's foot, his hand was an eagle's talon. He fell on me and his claws were in my hair, he held me fast and I smothered; then he transformed me so that my arms became wings covered with feathers. He turned his stare towards me, and he led me away to the palace of Irkalla, the Queen of Darkness, to the house from which none who enters ever returns, down the road from which there is no coming back.

'There is the house whose people sit in darkness; dust is their food and clay their meat. They are clothed like birds with wings for covering, they see no light, they sit in darkness. I entered the house of dust and I saw the kings of the earth, their crowns put away for ever; rulers and princes, all those who once wore kingly crowns and ruled the world in the days of old. They who had stood in the place of the gods like Anu and Enlil, stood now like servants to fetch baked meats in the house of dust, to carry cooked meat and cold water from the water-skin. In the house of dust which I entered were high priests and acolytes, priests of the incantation and of ecstasy; there were servers of the temple, and there was Etana, that king of Kish whom the eagle carried to heaven in the days of old. I saw also Samuqan, god of cattle, and there was Ereshkigal the Queen of the Underworld; and Belit-Sheri squatted in front of her, she who is recorder of the gods and keeps the book of death. She held a tablet from which she read. She raised her head, she saw me and spoke: "Who has brought this one here?" Then I awoke like a man drained of blood who wanders alone in a waste of rushes; like one whom the bailiff has seized and his heart pounds with terror.'

Gilgamesh had peeled off his clothes, he listened to his words and wept quick tears, Gilgamesh listened and his tears flowed. He opened his mouth and spoke to Enkidu: 'Who is there in strong-walled Uruk who has wisdom like this? Strange things have been spoken, why does your heart speak strangely? The dream was marvellous but the terror was great; we must treasure the dream whatever the terror; for the dream has shown that misery comes at last to the healthy man, the end of life is sorrow.' And Gilgamesh lamented, 'Now I will pray to the great gods, for my friend had an ominous dream.'

This day on which Enkidu dreamed came to an end and he lay stricken with sickness. One whole day he lay on his bed and his suffering increased. He said to Gilgamesh, the friend on whose account he had left the wilderness, 'Once I ran for you, for the water of life, and

I now have nothing.' A second day he lay on his bed and Gilgamesh watched over him but the sickness increased. A third day he lay on his bed, he called out to Gilgamesh, rousing him up. Now he was weak and his eyes were blind with weeping. Ten days he lay and his suffering increased, eleven and twelve days he lay on his bed of pain. Then he called to Gilgamesh, 'My friend, the great goddess cursed me and I must die in shame. I shall not die like a man fallen in battle; I feared to fall, but happy is the man who falls in the battle, for I must die in shame.' And Gilgamesh wept over Enkidu. With the first light of dawn he raised his voice and said to the counsellors of Uruk:

'Hear me, great ones of Uruk,
I weep for Enkidu, my friend,
Bitterly moaning like a woman mourning
I weep for my brother.
O Enkidu, my brother,
You were the axe at my side,
My hand's strength, the sword in my belt,
The shield before me,
A glorious robe, my fairest ornament;
An evil Fate has robbed me.
The wild ass and the gazelle
That were father and mother,
All long-tailed creatures that nourished you
Weep for you,
All the wild things of the plain and pastures;
The paths that you loved in the forest of cedars
Night and day murmur.

Let the great ones of strong-walled Uruk
Weep for you;
Let the finger of blessing
Be stretched out in mourning;
Enkidu, young brother. Hark,
There is an echo through all the country
Like a mother mourning.
Weep all the paths where we walked together;
And the beasts we hunted, the bear and hyena,
Tiger and panther, leopard and lion,
The stag and the ibex, the bull and the doe.
The river along whose banks we used to walk,
Weeps for you,
Ula of Elam and dear Euphrates
Where once we drew water for the water-skins.
The mountain we climbed where we slew the Watchman,
Weeps for you.
The warriors of strong-walled Uruk
Where the Bull of Heaven was killed,
Weep for you.
All the people of Eridu
Weep for you Enkidu.
Those who brought grain for your eating
Mourn for you now;
Who rubbed oil on your back
Mourn for you now;
Who poured beer for your drinking
Mourn for you now.
The harlot who anointed you with fragrant ointment
Laments for you now;
The women of the palace, who brought you a wife,

A chosen ring of good advice,
Lament for you now.
And the young men your brothers
As though they were women
Go long-haired in mourning.
What is this sleep which holds you now?
You are lost in the dark and cannot hear me.'

He touched his heart but it did not beat, nor did he lift his eyes again. When Gilgamesh touched his heart it did not beat. So Gilgamesh laid a veil, as one veils the bride, over his friend. He began to rage like a lion, like a lioness robbed of her whelps. This way and that he paced round the bed, he tore out his hair and strewed it around. He dragged off his splendid robes and flung them down as though they were abominations.

In the first light of dawn Gilgamesh cried out, 'I made you rest on a royal bed, you reclined on a couch at my left hand, the princes of the earth kissed your feet. I will cause all the people of Uruk to weep over you and raise the dirge of the dead. The joyful people will stoop with sorrow; and when you have gone to the earth I will let my hair grow long for your sake, I will wander through the wilderness in the skin of a lion.' The next day also, in the first light, Gilgamesh lamented; seven days and seven nights he wept for Enkidu, until the worm fastened on him. Only then he gave him up to the earth, for the Anunnaki, the judges, had seized him.

Then Gilgamesh issued a proclamation through the land, he summoned them all, the coppersmiths, the goldsmiths, the stone-workers, and commanded them, 'Make a statue of my friend.' The statue was fashioned with a great weight of lapis lazuli for the breast and of gold for the body. A table of hard-wood was set out, and on it a bowl of carnelian filled with honey, and a bowl of lapis lazuli filled with butter. These he exposed and offered to the Sun; and weeping he went away.

4

The Search for Everlasting Life

Bitterly Gilgamesh wept for his friend Enkidu; he wandered over the wilderness as a hunter, he roamed over the plains; in his bitterness he cried, 'How can I rest, how can I be at peace? Despair is in my heart. What my brother is now, that shall I be when I am dead. Because I am afraid of death I will go as best I can to find Utnapishtim whom they call the Faraway, for he has entered the assembly of the gods.' So Gilgamesh travelled over the wilderness, he wandered over the grasslands, a long journey, in search of Utnapishtim, whom the gods took after the deluge; and they set him to live in the land of Dilmun, in the garden of the sun; and to him alone of men they gave everlasting life.

At night when he came to the mountain passes Gilgamesh prayed: 'In these mountain passes long ago I saw lions, I was afraid and I lifted my eyes to the moon; I prayed and my prayers went up to the gods, so now, O moon god Sin, protect me.' When he had prayed he lay down to sleep, until he was woken from out of a dream. He saw the lions round him glorying in life; then he took his axe in his hand, he drew his sword from his belt, and he fell upon them like an arrow from the string, and struck and destroyed and scattered them.

So at length Gilgamesh came to Mashu, the great mountains about which he had heard many things, which guard the rising and the setting sun. Its twin peaks are as high as the wall of heaven and its paps reach down to the underworld. At its gate the Scorpions stand guard, half man and half dragon; their glory is terrifying, their stare strikes death into men, their shimmering halo sweeps the mountains that guard the rising sun. When Gilgamesh saw them he shielded his eyes for the length of a moment only; then he took courage and approached. When they saw him so undismayed the Man-Scorpion called to his mate, 'This one who comes to us now is flesh of the gods.' The mate of the Man-Scorpion answered, 'Two thirds is god but one third is man.'

Then he called to the man Gilgamesh, he called to the child of the gods: 'Why have you come so great a journey; for what have you travelled so far, crossing the dangerous waters; tell me the reason for your coming?' Gilgamesh answered, 'For Enkidu; I loved him dearly, together we endured all kinds of hardships; on his account I have come, for the common lot of man has taken him. I have wept for him day and night, I would not give up his body for burial, I thought my friend would come back because of my weeping. Since he went, my life is nothing; that is why I have travelled here in search of Utnapishtim my father; for men say he has entered the assembly of the gods, and has found everlasting life. I have a desire to question him concerning the living and the dead.' The Man-Scorpion opened his mouth and said, speaking to Gilgamesh, 'No man born of woman has done what you have asked, no mortal man has gone into the mountain; the length of it is twelve leagues of darkness; in it there is no light, but the heart is oppressed with darkness. From the rising of the sun to the setting of the sun there is no light.' Gilgamesh said, 'Although I should go in sorrow and in pain, with sighing and with weeping, still I must go. Open the gate of the mountain.' And the Man-Scorpion said, 'Go, Gilgamesh, I permit you to pass through the mountain of Mashu and through the high ranges; may your feet carry you safely home. The gate of the mountain is open.'

When Gilgamesh heard this he did as the Man-Scorpion had said, he followed the sun's road to his rising, through the mountain. When he had gone one league the darkness became thick around him, for there was no light, he could see nothing ahead and nothing behind him. After two leagues the darkness was thick and there was no light, he could see nothing ahead and nothing behind him. After three leagues the darkness was thick, and there was no light, he could see nothing ahead and nothing behind him. After four leagues the darkness was thick and there was no light, he could see nothing ahead and nothing behind him. At the end of five leagues the darkness was thick and there was no light, he could see nothing ahead and nothing behind him. At the end of six leagues the darkness was thick and there was no light, he could see nothing ahead and nothing behind him. When he had gone seven leagues the darkness was thick and there was no light, he could see nothing ahead and nothing behind him. When he had gone eight leagues Gilgamesh gave a great cry, for the darkness was thick and he could see nothing ahead and nothing behind him. After nine leagues he felt the north wind on his face, but the darkness was thick and there was no light, he could see nothing ahead and nothing behind him. After ten leagues the end was near. After eleven leagues the dawn light appeared. At the end of twelve leagues the sun streamed out.

There was the garden of the gods; all round him stood bushes bearing gems. Seeing it he went down at once, for there was fruit of carnelian with the vine hanging from it, beautiful to look at; lapis lazuli leaves hung thick with fruit, sweet to see. For thorns and thistles there were haematite and rare stones, agate, and pearls from out of the sea. While Gilgamesh walked in the garden by the edge of the sea Shamash saw him, and he saw that he was dressed in the skins of animals and ate their flesh. He was distressed, and he spoke and said, 'No mortal man has gone this way before, nor will, as long as the winds drive over the sea.' And to Gilgamesh he said, 'You will never find the life for which you are searching.' Gilgamesh said to glorious Shamash, 'Now that I have toiled and strayed so far over the wilderness, am I to sleep, and let the earth cover my head for ever? Let my eyes see the sun until they are dazzled with looking. Although I am no better than a dead man, still let me see the light of the sun.'

Beside the sea she lives, the woman of the vine, the maker of wine; Siduri sits in the garden at the edge of the sea, with the golden bowl and the golden vats that the gods gave her. She is covered with a veil; and where she sits she sees Gilgamesh coming towards her, wearing skins, the flesh of the gods in his body, but despair in his heart, and his face like the face of one who has made a long journey. She looked, and as she scanned the distance she said in her own heart, 'Surely this is some felon; where is he going now?' And she barred her gate against him with the cross-bar and shot home the bolt. But Gilgamesh, hearing the sound of the bolt, threw up his head and lodged his foot in the gate; he called to her, 'Young woman, maker of wine, why do you bolt your door; what did you see that made you bar your gate? I will break in your door and burst in your gate, for I am Gilgamesh who seized and killed the Bull of Heaven, I killed the watchman of the cedar forest, I overthrew Humbaba who lived in the forest, and I killed the lions in the passes of the mountain.'

Then Siduri said to him, 'If you are that Gilgamesh who seized and killed the Bull of Heaven, who killed the watchman of the cedar forest, who overthrew Humbaba that lived in the forest, and killed the lions in the passes of the mountain, why are your cheeks so starved and why is your face so drawn? Why is despair in your heart and your face like the face of one who has made a long journey? Yes, why is your face burned from heat and cold, and why do you come here wandering over the pastures in search of the wind?'

Gilgamesh answered her, 'And why should not my cheeks be starved and my face drawn? Despair is in my heart and my face is the face of one who has made a long journey, it was burned with heat and with cold. Why should I not wander over the pastures in search of the wind? My friend, my younger brother, he who hunted the wild ass of the wilderness and the panther of the plains, my friend, my younger brother who seized and killed the Bull of Heaven and overthrew Humbaba in the cedar forest, my friend who was very dear to me and who endured dangers beside me, Enkidu my brother, whom I loved, the end of mortality has overtaken him. I wept for him seven days and nights till the worm fastened on him. Because of my brother I am afraid of death, because of my brother I stray through the wilderness and cannot rest. But now, young woman, maker of wine, since I have seen your face do not let me see the face of death which I dread so much.'

She answered, 'Gilgamesh, where are you hurrying to? You will never find that life for which you are looking. When the gods created man they allotted to him death, but life they retained in their own keeping. As for you, Gilgamesh, fill your belly with good things; day and night, night and day, dance and be merry, feast and rejoice. Let your clothes be fresh, bathe yourself in water, cherish the little child that holds your hand, and make your wife happy in your embrace; for this too is the lot of man.'

But Gilgamesh said to Siduri, the young woman, 'How can I be silent, how can I rest, when Enkidu whom I love is dust, and I too shall die and be laid in the earth. You live by the sea-shore and look into the heart of it; young woman, tell me now, which is the way to Utnapishtim, the son of Ubara-Tutu? What directions are there for the passage; give me, oh, give me directions. I will cross the Ocean if it is possible; if it is not I will wander still farther in the wilderness.' The wine-maker said to him, 'Gilgamesh, there is no crossing the Ocean; whoever has come, since the days of old, has not been able to pass that sea. The Sun in his glory crosses the Ocean, but who beside Shamash has ever crossed it? The place and the passage are difficult, and the waters of death are deep which flow between. Gilgamesh, how will you cross the Ocean? When you come to the waters of death what will you do? But Gilgamesh, down in the woods you will find Urshanabi, the ferryman of Utnapishtim; with him are the holy things, the things of stone. He is fashioning the serpent prow of the boat. Look at him well, and if it is possible, perhaps you will cross the waters with him; but if it is not possible, then you must go back.'

When Gilgamesh heard this he was seized with anger. He took his axe in his hand, and his dagger from his belt. He crept forward and he fell on them like a javelin. Then he went into the forest and sat down. Urshanabi saw the dagger flash and heard the axe, and he beat his head, for Gilgamesh had shattered the tackle of the boat in his rage. Urshanabi said to him, 'Tell me, what is your name? I am Urshanabi, the ferryman of Utnapishtim the Faraway.' He replied to him, 'Gilgamesh is my name, I am from Uruk, from the house of Anu.' Then Urshanabi said to him, 'Why are your cheeks so starved and your face drawn? Why is despair in your heart and your face like the face of one who has made a long journey; yes, why is your face burned with heat and with cold, and why do you come here wandering over the pastures in search of the wind?'

Gilgamesh said to him, 'Why should not my cheeks be starved and my face drawn? Despair is in my heart, and my face is the face of one who has made a long journey. I was burned with heat and with cold. Why should I not wander over the pastures? My friend, my younger brother who seized and killed the Bull of Heaven, and overthrew Humbaba in the cedar forest, my friend who was very dear to me, and who endured dangers beside me, Enkidu my brother whom I loved, the end of mortality has overtaken him. I wept for him seven days and nights till the worm fastened on him. Because of my brother I am afraid of death, because of my brother I stray through the wilderness. His fate lies heavy upon me. How can I be silent, how can I rest? He is dust and I too shall die and be laid in the earth for ever. I am afraid of death, therefore, Urshanabi, tell me which is the road to Utnapishtim? If it is possible I will cross the waters of death; if not I will wander still farther through the wilderness.'

Urshanabi said to him, 'Gilgamesh, your own hands have prevented you from crossing the Ocean; when you destroyed the tackle of the boat you destroyed its safety.' Then the two of them talked it over and Gilgamesh said, 'Why are you so angry with me, Urshanabi, for you yourself cross the sea by day and night, at all seasons you cross it.' 'Gilgamesh, those things you destroyed, their property is to carry me over the water, to prevent the waters of death from touching me. It was for this reason that I preserved them, but you have destroyed them, and the *urnu* snakes with them. But now, go into the forest, Gilgamesh; with your axe cut poles, one hundred and twenty, cut them sixty cubits long, paint them with bitumen, set on them ferrules and bring them back.'

When Gilgamesh heard this he went into the forest, he cut poles one hundred and twenty; he cut them sixty cubits long, he painted them with bitumen, he set on them ferrules, and he brought them to Urshanabi. Then they boarded the boat, Gilgamesh and Urshanabi together, launching it out on the waves of the Ocean. For three days they ran on as it were a journey of a month and fifteen days, and at last Urshanabi brought the boat to the waters of death. Then Urshanabi said to Gilgamesh, 'Press on, take a pole and thrust it in, but do not let your hands touch the waters. Gilgamesh, take a second pole, take a third, take a fourth pole. Now, Gilgamesh, take a fifth, take a sixth and seventh pole. Gilgamesh, take an eighth, and ninth, a tenth pole. Gilgamesh, take an eleventh, take a twelfth pole.' After one hundred and twenty thrusts Gilgamesh had used the last pole. Then he stripped himself, he held up his arms for a mast and his covering for a sail. So Urshanabi the ferryman brought Gilgamesh to Utnapishtim, whom they call the Faraway, who lives in Dilmun at the place of the sun's transit, eastward of the mountain. To him alone of men the gods had given everlasting life.

Now Utnapishtim, where he lay at ease, looked into the distance and he said in his heart, musing to himself, 'Why does the boat sail here without tackle and mast; why are the sacred stones destroyed, and why does the master not sail the boat? That man who comes is none of mine; where I look I see a man whose body is covered with skins of beasts. Who is this who walks up the shore behind Urshanabi, for surely he is no man of mine?' So Utnapishtim looked at him and said, 'What is your name, you who come here wearing the skins of beasts, with your cheeks starved and your face drawn? Where are you hurrying to now? For what reason have you made this great journey, crossing the seas whose passage is difficult? Tell me the reason for your coming.'

He replied, 'Gilgamesh is my name. I am from Uruk, from the house of Anu.' Then Utnapishtim said to him, 'If you are Gilgamesh, why are your cheeks so starved and your face drawn? Why is despair in your heart and your face like the face of one who has made a long journey? Yes, why is your face burned with heat and cold; and why do you come here, wandering over the wilderness in search of the wind?'

Gilgamesh said to him, 'Why should not my cheeks be starved and my face drawn? Despair is in my heart and my face is the face of one who has made a long journey. It was burned with heat and with cold. Why should I not wander over the pastures? My friend, my younger brother who seized and killed the Bull of Heaven and overthrew Humbaba in the cedar forest, my friend who was very dear to me and endured dangers beside me, Enkidu, my brother whom I loved, the end of mortality has overtaken him. I wept for him seven days and nights till the worm fastened on him. Because of my brother I am afraid of death; because of my brother I stray through the wilderness. His fate lies heavy upon me. How can I be silent, how can I rest? He is dust and I shall die also and be laid in the earth for ever.' Again Gilgamesh said, speaking to Utnapishtim, 'It is to see Utnapishtim whom we call the Faraway that I have come this journey. For this I have wandered over the world,

I have crossed many difficult ranges, I have crossed the seas, I have wearied myself with travelling; my joints are aching, and I have lost acquaintance with sleep which is sweet. My clothes were worn out before I came to the house of Siduri. I have killed the bear and hyena, the lion and panther, the tiger, the stag and the ibex, all sorts of wild game and the small creatures of the pastures. I ate their flesh and I wore their skins; and that was how I came to the gate of the young woman, the maker of wine, who barred her gate of pitch and bitumen against me. But from her I had news of the journey; so then I came to Urshanabi the ferryman, and with him I crossed over the waters of death. Oh, father Utnapishtim, you who have entered the assembly of the gods, I wish to question you concerning the living and the dead, how shall I find the life for which I am searching?'

Utnapishtim said, 'There is no permanence. Do we build a house to stand for ever, do we seal a contract to hold for all time? Do brothers divide an inheritance to keep for ever, does the flood-time of rivers endure? It is only the nymph of the dragon-fly who sheds her larva and sees the sun in his glory. From the days of old there is no permanence. The sleeping and the dead, how alike they are, they are like a painted death. What is there between the master and the servant when both have fulfilled their doom? When the Anunnaki, the judges, come together, and Mammetun the mother of destinies, together they decree the fates of men. Life and death they allot but the day of death they do not disclose.'

Then Gilgamesh said to Utnapishtim the Faraway, 'I look at you now, Utnapishtim, and your appearance is no different from mine; there is nothing strange in your features. I thought I should find you like a hero prepared for battle, but you lie here taking your ease on your back. Tell me truly, how was it that you came to enter the company of the gods and to possess everlasting life?' Utnapishtim said to Gilgamesh, 'I will reveal to you a mystery, I will tell you a secret of the gods.'

5

The Story of the Flood

'You know the city Shurrupak, it stands on the banks of
Euphrates? That city grew old and the gods that were in
it were old. There was Anu, lord of the firmament, their
father, and warrior Enlil their counsellor, Ninurta the
helper, and Ennugi watcher over canals; and with them
also was Ea. In those days the world teemed, the people
multiplied, the world bellowed like a wild bull, and the
great god was aroused by the clamour. Enlil heard the
clamour and he said to the gods in council, "The uproar
of mankind is intolerable and sleep is no longer possible
by reason of the babel." So the gods agreed to extermi-
nate mankind. Enlil did this, but Ea because of his oath
warned me in a dream. He whispered their words to my
house of reeds, "Reed-house, reed-house! Wall, O wall,
hearken reed-house, wall reflect; O man of Shurrupak,
son of Ubara-Tutu; tear down your house and build a
boat, abandon possessions and look for life, despise
worldly goods and save your soul alive. Tear down your
house, I say, and build a boat. These are the measure-
ments of the barque as you shall build her: let her beam
equal her length, let her deck be roofed like the vault
that covers the abyss; then take up into the boat the seed
of all living creatures."

'When I had understood I said to my lord, "Behold,
what you have commanded I will honour and perform,

but how shall I answer the people, the city, the elders?"
Then Ea opened his mouth and said to me, his servant,
"Tell them this: I have learnt that Enlil is wrathful against
me, I dare no longer walk in his land nor live in his city;
I will go down to the Gulf to dwell with Ea my lord. But
on you he will rain down abundance, rare fish and shy
wild-fowl, a rich harvest-tide. In the evening the rider of
the storm will bring you wheat in torrents."

'In the first light of dawn all my household gathered
round me, the children brought pitch and the men what-
ever was necessary. On the fifth day I laid the keel and
the ribs, then I made fast the planking. The ground-space
was one acre, each side of the deck measured one hun-
dred and twenty cubits, making a square. I built six decks
below, seven in all, I divided them into nine sections with
bulkheads between. I drove in wedges where needed, I
saw to the punt-poles, and laid in supplies. The carriers
brought oil in baskets, I poured pitch into the furnace
and asphalt and oil; more oil was consumed in caulking,
and more again the master of the boat took into his
stores. I slaughtered bullocks for the people and every
day I killed sheep. I gave the shipwrights wine to drink
as though it were river water, raw wine and red wine
and oil and white wine. There was feasting then as there
is at the time of the New Year's festival; I myself anointed
my head. On the seventh day the boat was complete.

'Then was the launching full of difficulty; there was
shifting of ballast above and below till two thirds was
submerged. I loaded into her all that I had of gold and
of living things, my family, my kin, the beast of the field
both wild and tame, and all the craftsmen. I sent them

on board, for the time that Shamash had ordained was already fulfilled when he said, "In the evening, when the rider of the storm sends down the destroying rain, enter the boat and batten her down." The time was fulfilled, the evening came, the rider of the storm sent down the rain. I looked out at the weather and it was terrible, so I too boarded the boat and battened her down. All was now complete, the battening and the caulking; so I handed the tiller to Puzur-Amurri the steersman, with the navigation and the care of the whole boat.

'With the first light of dawn a black cloud came from the horizon; it thundered within where Adad, lord of the storm was riding. In front over hill and plain Shullat and Hanish, heralds of the storm, led on. Then the gods of the abyss rose up; Nergal pulled out the dams of the nether waters, Ninurta the war-lord threw down the dykes, and the seven judges of hell, the Annunaki, raised their torches, lighting the land with their livid flame. A stupor of despair went up to heaven when the god of the storm turned daylight to darkness, when he smashed the land like a cup. One whole day the tempest raged, gathering fury as it went, it poured over the people like the tides of battle; a man could not see his brother nor the people be seen from heaven. Even the gods were terrified at the flood, they fled to the highest heaven, the firmament of Anu; they crouched against the walls, cowering like curs. Then Ishtar the sweet-voiced Queen of Heaven cried out like a woman in travail: "Alas the days of old are turned to dust because I commanded evil; why did I command this evil in the council of all the gods? I commanded wars to destroy the people, but are they not my people, for I brought them forth? Now like the spawn of fish they float in the ocean.'' The great gods of heaven and of hell wept, they covered their mouths.

'For six days and six nights the winds blew, torrent and tempest and flood overwhelmed the world, tempest and flood raged together like warring hosts. When the seventh day dawned the storm from the south subsided, the sea grew calm, the flood was stilled; I looked at the face of the world and there was silence, all mankind was turned to clay. The surface of the sea stretched as flat as a roof-top; I opened a hatch and the light fell on my face. Then I bowed low, I sat down and I wept, the tears streamed down my face, for on every side was the waste of water. I looked for land in vain, but fourteen leagues distant there appeared a mountain, and there the boat grounded; on the mountain of Nisir the boat held fast, she held fast and did not budge. One day she held, and a second day on the mountain of Nisir she held fast and did not budge. A third day, and a fourth day she held fast on the mountain and did not budge; a fifth day and a sixth day she held fast on the mountain. When the seventh day dawned I loosed a dove and let her go. She flew away, but finding no resting-place she returned. Then I loosed a swallow, and she flew away but finding no resting-place she returned. I loosed a raven, she saw that the waters had retreated, she ate, she flew around, she cawed, and she did not come back. Then I threw everything open to the four winds, I made a sacrifice and poured out a libation on the mountain top. Seven and again seven cauldrons I set up on their stands, I heaped up wood and cane and cedar and myrtle. When the gods smelled the sweet savour, they gathered like flies over the sacrifice. Then, at last, Ishtar also came, she lifted her necklace with the jewels of heaven that once Anu had made to please her. "O you gods here present, by the lapis lazuli round my neck I shall remember these days as I remember the jewels of my throat; these last days I shall not forget. Let all the gods gather round the sacrifice, except Enlil. He shall not approach this offering, for without reflection he brought the flood; he consigned my people to destruction."

'When Enlil had come, when he saw the boat, he was wrath and swelled with anger at the gods, the host of heaven, "Has any of these mortals escaped? Not one was to have survived the destruction." Then the god of the wells and canals Ninurta opened his mouth and said to the warrior Enlil, "Who is there of the gods that can devise without Ea? It is Ea alone who knows all things." Then Ea opened his mouth and spoke to warrior Enlil, "Wisest of gods, hero Enlil, how could you so senselessly bring down the flood?

> Lay upon the sinner his sin,
> Lay upon the transgressor his transgression,
> Punish him a little when he breaks loose,
> Do not drive him too hard or he perishes;
> Would that a lion had ravaged mankind
> Rather than the flood,
> Would that a wolf had ravaged mankind
> Rather than the flood,
> Would that famine had wasted the world

Rather than the flood,
Would that pestilence had wasted mankind
Rather than the flood.

It was not I that revealed the secret of the gods; the wise man learned it in a dream. Now take your counsel what shall be done with him."

'Then Enlil went up into the boat, he took me by the hand and my wife and made us enter the boat and kneel down on either side, he standing between us. He touched our foreheads to bless us, saying, "In time past Utnapishtim was a mortal man; henceforth he and his wife shall live in the distance at the mouth of the rivers." Thus it was that the gods took me and placed me here to live in the distance, at the mouth of the rivers.'

6

The Return

Utnapishtim said, 'As for you, Gilgamesh, who will assemble the gods for your sake, so that you may find that life for which you are searching? But if you wish, come and put it to the test: only prevail against sleep for six days and seven nights.' But while Gilgamesh sat there resting on his haunches, a mist of sleep like soft wool teased from the fleece drifted over him, and Utnapishtim said to his wife, 'Look at him now, the strong man who would have everlasting life, even now the mists of sleep are drifting over him.' His wife replied, 'Touch the man to wake him, so that he may return to his own land in peace, going back through the gate by which he came.' Utnapishtim said to his wife, 'All men are deceivers, even you he will attempt to deceive; therefore bake loaves of bread, each day one loaf, and put it beside his head; and make a mark on the wall to number the days he has slept.'

So she baked loaves of bread, each day one loaf, and put it beside his head, and she marked on the wall the days that he slept; and there came a day when the first loaf was hard, the second loaf was like leather, the third was soggy, the crust of the fourth had mould, the fifth was mildewed, the sixth was fresh, and the seventh was still on the embers. Then Utnapishtim touched him and he woke. Gilgamesh said to Utnapishtim the Faraway, 'I hardly slept when you touched and roused me.' But Utnapishtim said, 'Count these loaves and learn how many days you slept, for your first is hard, your second like leather, your third is soggy, the crust of your fourth has mould, your fifth is mildewed, your sixth is fresh and your seventh was still over the glowing embers when I touched and woke you.' Gilgamesh said, 'What shall I do, O Utnapishtim, where shall I go? Already the thief in the night has hold of my limbs, death inhabits my room; wherever my foot rests, there I find death.'

Then Utnapishtim spoke to Urshanabi the ferryman: 'Woe to you Urshanabi, now and for ever more you have become hateful to this harbourage; it is not for you, nor for you are the crossings of this sea. Go now, banished from the shore. But this man before whom you walked, bringing him here, whose body is covered with foulness and the grace of whose limbs has been spoiled by wild skins, take him to the washing-place. There he shall wash his long hair clean as snow in the water, he shall throw off his skins and let the sea carry them away, and the beauty of his body shall be shown, the fillet on his forehead shall be renewed, and he shall be given clothes to cover his nakedness. Till he reaches his own city and his journey is accomplished, these clothes will show no sign of age, they will wear like a new garment.' So Urshanabi took Gilgamesh and led him to the washing-place, he washed his long hair as clean as snow in the water, he threw off his skins, which the sea carried away, and showed the beauty of his body. He renewed the fillet on his forehead, and to cover his nakedness gave him clothes which would show no sign of age, but would wear like a new garment till he reached his own city, and his journey was accomplished.

Then Gilgamesh and Urshanabi launched the boat on to the water and boarded it, and they made ready to sail away; but the wife of Utnapishtim the Faraway said to him, 'Gilgamesh came here wearied out, he is worn out; what will you give him to carry him back to his own country?' So Utnapishtim spoke, and Gilgamesh took a pole and brought the boat in to the bank. 'Gilgamesh, you came here a man wearied out, you have worn yourself out; what shall I give you to carry you back to your own country? Gilgamesh, I shall reveal a secret thing, it is a mystery of the gods that I am telling you. There is a plant that grows under the water, it has a prickle like a thorn, like a rose; it will wound your hands, but if you succeed in taking it, then your hands will hold that which restores his lost youth to a man.'

When Gilgamesh heard this he opened the sluices so that a sweet-water current might carry him out to the deepest channel; he tied heavy stones to his feet and they dragged him down to the water-bed. There he saw the plant growing; although it pricked him he took it in his hands; then he cut the heavy stones from his feet, and the sea carried him and threw him on to the shore. Gilgamesh said to Urshanabi the ferryman, 'Come here, and see this marvellous plant. By its virtue a man may win back all his former strength. I will take it to Uruk of the strong walls; there I will give it to the old men to eat. Its name shall be "The Old Men Are Young Again"; and at last I shall eat it myself and have back all my lost youth.' So Gilgamesh returned by the gate through which he had come, Gilgamesh and Urshanabi went together. They travelled their twenty leagues and then they broke their fast; after thirty leagues they stopped for the night.

Gilgamesh saw a well of cool water and he went down and bathed; but deep in the pool there was lying a serpent, and the serpent sensed the sweetness of the flower. It rose out of the water and snatched it away, and immediately it sloughed its skin and returned to the well. Then Gilgamesh sat down and wept, the tears ran down his face, and he took the hand of Urshanabi; 'O Urshanabi, was it for this that I toiled with my hands, is it for this I have wrung out my heart's blood? For myself I have gained nothing; not I, but the beast of the earth has joy of it now. Already the stream has carried it twenty leagues back to the channels where I found it. I found a sign and now I have lost it. Let us leave the boat on the bank and go.'

After twenty leagues they broke their fast, after thirty leagues they stopped for the night; in three days they had walked as much as a journey of a month and fifteen days. When the journey was accomplished they arrived at Uruk, the strong-walled city. Gilgamesh spoke to him, to Urshanabi the ferryman, 'Urshanabi, climb up on to the wall of Uruk, inspect its foundation terrace, and examine well the brickwork; see if it is not of burnt bricks; and did not the seven wise men lay these foundations? One third of the whole is city, one third is garden, and one third is field, with the precinct of the goddess Ishtar. These parts and the precinct are all Uruk.'

This too was the work of Gilgamesh, the king, who

knew the countries of the world. He was wise, he saw
mysteries and knew secret things, he brought us a tale
of the days before the flood. He went a long journey, was
weary, worn out with labour, and returning engraved on
a stone the whole story.

The Death of Gilgamesh

The destiny was fulfilled which the father of the gods, Enlil of the mountain, had decreed for Gilgamesh: 'In nether-earth the darkness will show him a light: of mankind, all that are known, none will leave a monument for generations to come to compare with his. The heroes, the wise men, like the new moon have their waxing and waning. Men will say, "Who has ever ruled with might and with power like him?" As in the dark month, the month of shadows, so without him there is no light. O Gilgamesh, this was the meaning of your dream. You were given the kingship, such was your destiny, everlasting life was not your destiny. Because of this do not be sad at heart, do not be grieved or oppressed; he has given you power to bind and to loose, to be the darkness and the light of mankind. He has given unexampled supremacy over the people, victory in battle from which no fugitive returns, in forays and assaults from which there is no going back. But do not abuse this power, deal justly with your servants in the palace, deal justly before the face of the Sun.'

The king has laid himself down and will not rise again,
The Lord of Kullab will not rise again;
He overcame evil, he will not come again;
Though he was strong of arm he will not rise again;

He had wisdom and a comely face, he will not come again;
He is gone into the mountain, he will not come again;
On the bed of fate he lies, he will not rise again,
From the couch of many colours he will not come again.

The people of the city, great and small, are not silent; they lift up the lament, all men of flesh and blood lift up the lament. Fate has spoken; like a hooked fish he lies stretched on the bed, like a gazelle that is caught in a noose. Inhuman Namtar is heavy upon him, Namtar that has neither hand nor foot, that drinks no water and eats no meat.

For Gilgamesh, son of Ninsun, they weighed out their offerings; his dear wife, his son, his concubine, his musicians, his jester, and all his household; his servants, his stewards, all who lived in the palace weighed out their offerings for Gilgamesh the son of Ninsun, the heart of Uruk. They weighed out their offerings to Ereshkigal, the Queen of Death, and to all the gods of the dead. To Namtar, who is fate, they weighed out the offering. Bread for Neti the Keeper of the Gate, bread for Ningizzida the god of the serpent, the lord of the Tree of Life; for Dumuzi also, the young shepherd, for Enki and Ninki, for Endukugga and Nindukugga, for Enmul and Ninmul, all the ancestral gods, forbears of Enlil. A feast for Shulpae the god of feasting. For Samuqan, god of the herds, for the mother Ninhursag, and the gods of creation in the place of creation, for the host of heaven, priest and priestess weighed out the offering of the dead.

Gilgamesh, the son of Ninsun, lies in the tomb. At the place of offerings he weighed the bread-offering, at the place of libation he poured out the wine. In those days the lord Gilgamesh departed, the son of Ninsun, the king, peerless, without an equal among men, who did not neglect Enlil his master. O Gilgamesh, lord of Kullab, great is thy praise.

Glossary of Names

A short description of the gods and of other persons and places mentioned in the Epic will be found in this Glossary. The gods were credited at different times with a variety of attributes and characteristics, sometimes contradictory; only such as are relevant to the material of the Gilgamesh Epic are given here.

ADAD: Storm-, rain-, and weather-god.

ANSHAN: A district of Elam in south-west Persia; probably the source of supplies of wood for making bows. Gilgamesh has a 'bow of Anshan'.

ANTUM: Wife of *Anu*.

ANU: Sumerian An; father of gods, and god of the firmament, the 'great above'. In the Sumerian cosmogony there was, first of all, the primeval sea, from which was born the cosmic mountain consisting of heaven, 'An', and earth, 'Ki'; they were separated by *Enlil*, then An carried off the heavens, and Enlil the earth. Anu later retreated more and more into the background; he had an important temple in Uruk.

ANUNNAKI: Usually gods of the underworld, judges of the dead and offspring of *Anu*.

APSU: The Abyss; the primeval waters under the earth; in the later mythology of the *Enuma Elish*, more particularly the sweet water which mingled with the bitter waters of the sea and with a third watery element, perhaps cloud, from which the first gods were engendered. The waters of Apsu were thought of as held immobile underground by the 'spell' of *Ea* in a death-like sleep.

ARURU: A goddess of creation, she created *Enkidu* from clay in the image of *Anu*.

AYA: The dawn, the bride of the Sun God *Shamash*.

BELIT-SHERI: Scribe and recorder of the underworld gods.

BULL OF HEAVEN: A personification of drought created by *Anu* for *Ishtar*.

DILMUN: The Sumerian paradise, perhaps the Persian Gulf, sometimes described as 'the place where the sun rises' and 'the Land of the Living'; the scene of a Sumerian creation myth and the place where the deified Sumerian hero of the flood, Ziusudra, was taken by the gods to live for ever.

DUMUZI: The Sumerian form of *Tammuz*; a god of vegetation and fertility, and so of the underworld, also called 'the Shepherd' and 'lord of the sheepfolds'. As the companion of *Ningizzida* 'to all eternity' he stands at the gate of heaven. In the Sumerian 'Descent of Inanna' he is the husband of the goddess Inanna, the Sumerian counterpart of *Ishtar*. According to the Sumerian King-List Gilgamesh was descended from 'Dumuzi a shepherd'.

EA: Sumerian Enki; god of the sweet waters, also of wisdom, a patron of arts and one of the creators of mankind, towards whom he is usually well-disposed. The chief god of Eridu, where he had a temple, he lived 'in the deep'; his ancestry is uncertain, but he was probably a child of *Anu*.

EANNA: The temple precinct in Uruk sacred to *Anu* and *Ishtar*.

EGALMAH: The 'Great Palace' in Uruk, the home of the goddess *Ninsun*, the mother of Gilgamesh.

ENDUKUGGA: With *Nindukugga*, Sumerian gods living in the underworld; parents of *Enlil*.

ENKIDU: Moulded by *Aruru*, goddess of creation, out of clay in the image and 'of the essence of *Anu*', the sky-god, and of *Ninurta* the war-god. The companion of Gilgamesh, he is wild or natural man; he was later considered a patron or god of animals and may have been the hero of another cycle.

ENLIL: God of earth, wind, and the universal air, ultimately spirit; the executive of *Anu*. In the Sumerian cosmogony he was born of the union of An heaven, and *Ki* earth. These he separated, and he then carried off earth as his portion. In later times he supplanted *Anu* as chief god. He was the patron of the city of Nippur.

ENMUL: See *Endukugga*.

ENNUGI: God of irrigation and inspector of canals.

ENUMA ELISH: The Semitic creation epic which describes the creation of the gods, the defeat of the powers of chaos by the young god Marduk, and the creation of man from the blood of Kingu, the defeated champion of chaos. The title is taken from the first words of the epic 'When on high'.

ERESHKIGAL: The Queen of the underworld, a counterpart of Persephone; probably once a sky-goddess. In the Sumerian cosmogony she was carried off to the underworld after the separation of heaven and earth.

ETANA: Legendary king of Kish who reigned after the flood; in the epic which bears his name he was carried to heaven on the back of an eagle.

GILGAMESH: The hero of the Epic; son of the goddess *Ninsun* and of a priest of *Kullab*, fifth king of Uruk after the flood, famous as a great builder and as a judge of the dead. A cycle of epic poems has collected round his name.

HANISH: A divine herald of storm and bad weather.

HUMBABA: Also Huwawa; a guardian of the cedar forest who opposes Gilgamesh and is killed by him and *Enkidu*. A nature divinity, perhaps an Anatolian, Elamite, or Syrian god.

IGIGI: Collective name for the great gods of heaven.

IRKALLA: Another name for *Ereshkigal*, the Queen of the underworld.

ISHTAR: Sumerian Inanna; the goddess of love and fertility, also goddess of war, called the Queen of Heaven. She is the daughter of *Anu* and patroness of *Uruk*, where she has a temple.

ISHULLANU: The gardener of *Anu*, once loved by *Ishtar*, whom he rejected; he was turned by her into a mole or frog.

KI: The earth.

KULLAB: Part of *Uruk*.

LUGULBANDA: Third king of the post-diluvian dynasty of Uruk, a god and shepherd, and hero of a cycle of Sumerian poems; protector of Gilgamesh.

MAGAN: A land to the west of Mesopotamia, sometimes Egypt or Arabia, and sometimes the land of the dead, the underworld.

MAGILUM: Uncertain meaning, perhaps 'the boat of the dead'.

MAMMETUN: Ancestral goddess responsible for destinies.

MAN-SCORPION: Guardian, with a similar female monster, of the mountain into which the sun descends at nightfall. Shown on sealings and ivory inlays as a figure with the upper part of the body human and the lower part ending in a scorpion's tail. According to the *Enuma Elish* created by the primeval waters in order to fight the gods.

MASHU: The word means 'twins' in the Akkadian language. A mountain with twin peaks into which the sun descends at nightfall and from which it returns at dawn. Sometimes thought of as Lebanon and Anti-Lebanon.

NAMTAR: Fate, destiny in its evil aspect; pictured as a demon of the underworld, also a messenger and chief minister of *Ereshkigal*; a bringer of disease and pestilence.

NEDU: See *Neti*.

NERGAL: Underworld god, sometimes the husband of *Ereshkigal*, he is the subject of an Akkadian poem which describes his translation from heaven to the underworld; plague-god.

NETI: The Sumerian form of *Nedu*, the chief gate-keeper in the underworld.

NINDUKUGGA: With *Endukugga*, parental gods living in the underworld.

NINGAL: Wife of the Moon God and mother of the Sun.

NINGIRSU: An earlier form of *Ninurta*; god of irrigation and fertility, he had a field near Lagash where all sorts of plants flourished; he was the child of a she-goat.

NINGIZZIDA: Also Gizzida; a fertility god, addressed as 'Lord of the Tree of Life'; sometimes he is a serpent with human head, but later he was a god of healing and magic; the companion of *Tammuz*, with whom he stood at the gate of heaven.

NINHURSAG: Sumerian mother-goddess; one of the four principal Sumerian gods with An, *Enlil*, and Enki; sometimes the wife of Enki, she created all vegetation. The name means 'the Mother'; she is also called 'Nintu', lady of birth, and *Ki*, the earth.

NINKI: The 'mother' of *Enlil*, probably a form of *Ninhursag*.

NINLIL: Goddess of heaven, earth, and air and in one aspect of the underworld; wife of *Enlil* and mother of the Moon; worshipped with Enlil in Nippur.

NINSUN: The mother of Gilgamesh, a minor goddess whose house was in Uruk; she was noted for wisdom, and was the wife of *Lugulbanda*.

NINURTA: The later form of *Ningirsu*; a warrior and god of war, a herald, the south wind, and god of wells and irrigation. According to one poem he once dammed up the bitter waters of the underworld and conquered various monsters.

NISABA: Goddess of grain.

NISIR: Probably means 'Mountain of Salvation'; sometimes identified with the Pir Oman Gudrun range south of the lower Zab, or with the biblical Ararat north of Lake Van.

PUZUR-AMURRI: The steersman of *Utnapishtim* during the flood.

SAMUQAN: God of cattle.

SEVEN SAGES: Wise men who brought civilization to the seven oldest cities of Mesopotamia.

SHAMASH: Sumerian Utu; the sun; for the Sumerians he was principally the judge and law-giver with some fertility attributes. For the Semites he was also a victorious warrior, the god of wisdom, the son of *Sin*, and 'greater than his father'. He was the husband and brother of *Ishtar*. He is represented with the saw with which he cuts decisions. In the poems 'Shamash' may mean the god, or simply the sun.

SHULLAT: A divine herald of storm and of bad weather.

SHULPAE: A god who presided over feasts and feasting.

SHURRUPAK: Modern Fara, eighteen miles north-west of Uruk; one of the oldest cities of Mesopotamia, and one of the five named by the Sumerians as having existed before the flood. The home of the hero of the flood story.

SIDURI: The divine wine-maker and brewer; she lives on the shore of the sea (perhaps the Mediterranean), in the garden of the sun. Her name in the Hurrian language means 'young woman' and she may be a form of *Ishtar*.

SILILI: The mother of the stallion; a divine mare?

SIN: Sumerian Nanna, the moon. The chief Sumerian astral deity, the father of Utu-*Shamash*, the sun, and of *Ishtar*. His parents were *Enlil* and *Ninlil*. His chief temple was in Ur.

TAMMUZ: Sumerian *Dumuzi*; the dying god of vegetation, bewailed by *Ishtar*, the subject of laments and litanies. In an Akkadian poem Ishtar descends to the underworld in search of her young husband Tammuz; but in the Sumerian poem on which this is based it is Inanna herself who is responsible for sending Dumuzi to the underworld because of his pride and as a hostage for her own safe return.

UBARA-TUTU: A king of *Shurrupak* and father of *Utnapishtim*. The only king of Kish named in the prediluvian King-List, apart from Utnapishtim.

URSHANABI: Old Babylonian Sursunabu; the boatman of *Utnapishtim* who ferries daily across the waters of death which divide the garden of the sun from the paradise where Utnapishtim lives for ever (the Sumerian *Dilmun*). By accepting Gilgamesh as a passenger he forfeits this right, and accompanies Gilgamesh back to *Uruk* instead.

URUK: Biblical Erech, modern Warka, in southern Babylonia between Fara (*Shurrupak*) and Ur. Shown by excavation to have been an important city from very early times, with great temples to the gods *Anu* and *Ishtar*. Traditionally the enemy of the city of Kish, and after the flood the seat of a dynasty of kings, among whom Gilgamesh was the fifth and most famous.

UTNAPISHTIM: Old Babylonian Utanapishtim, Sumerian Ziusudra; in the Sumerian poems he is a wise king and priest of *Shurrupak*; in the Akkadian sources he is a wise citizen of Shurrupak. He is the son of *Ubara-Tutu*, and his name is usually translated, 'He Who Saw Life'. He is the protégé of the god *Ea*, by whose connivance he survives the flood, with his family and with 'the seed of all living creatures'; afterwards he is taken by the gods to live for ever at 'the mouth of the rivers' and given the epithet 'Faraway'; or according to the Sumerians he lives in *Dilmun* where the sun rises.